Finding Real Love in Italy

Grenita Hall

ISBN: 978-1-955312-42-4

Printed in the United States of America
Story Corner Publishing & Consulting, Inc.
1510 Atlanta Ave.
Portsmouth, VA 23704

Storycornerpublishing@yahoo.com

www.StoryCornerPublishing.com

Dedication

I dedicate this book to my baby sister, Tryphenia Smith. I chose you because I remember watching you endure a lot of hardship when you were younger, and I admired your strength. Know that you will always hold a special place in my heart. I love you.

Table Of Content

Introduction

In this romance novel, I will take you on a journey of love that God has blessed me to share with you all. It takes place in Philadelphia, Pennsylvania, and transitions to Sicily, Italy, where a young girl named Lily Russo is abandoned by her parents and forced to live in Italy with her grandmother. As she gets older, she realizes a part of herself is missing. Lily desires to find love, hoping to fill the gaps of her broken heart. She desperately yawned for a savior because loneliness was suffocating her. Therefore, Lily goes on a quest for Mr. Right, praying to be swept off her feet and live happily ever after.

Sit back, grab a cup of coffee, tea, or whatever relaxes you and watch how it all unravels. I pray you all are blessed and find true love and happiness as a result of joining me on this journey.

CHAPTER 1

How Things Change

It was a warm and beautiful day in the city of Philadelphia. Mom and dad were relaxing in the living room. I played with my dolls, watching mother and father laugh as they held a conversation with each other. They then began to flirt and kiss one another. It was so lovely to see them both in love with each other.

My Father's name is Roberto Russo, and he is Italian. My mother's name is Sylvia Russo, and she is one of the most beautiful women I have ever seen. My mother met my dad in Italy back in 1987. They moved to Philadelphia, Pennsylvania, and got married. I was conceived years later. They said they wanted to enjoy their life together before they had children. I was just happy to have a chance at life. My name is Lily Russo. I was the only child. It was great to be five years old and spoiled. I got anything I wanted from my dad. I was his little princess, and no one could ever take my place. No one! Well, that was what I thought. I started noticing a change in my mother and father's intimacy. I was five years old but mature-minded. Therefore, I picked up on a lot. They could not get much past me.

My mother's attitude changed towards my father. They began to argue a lot, which made me sad because they usually always got along. Before the arguments, it looked as if nothing bothered them, and they were happy. I wanted to get to the bottom of it once and for all. I needed answers. We loved doing things together as a family, like eating together, watching movies, and playing cards that suddenly stopped! My mother loved to go out shopping for the house. Dad was more laid back and easy-going. He would give mother the credit card, and she would do her thing. Mother had money but never had to spend it at all. Dad tried his best to take care of us, but things surprisingly changed.

One day it happened! The most dreadful day that changed our lives forever. My dad and mother said they were getting a divorce. My heart broke into tiny pieces. I was devastated. I began to cry uncontrollably. My dad said it was for the best. I couldn't understand why he didn't want to fight to save their marriage. Maybe he didn't love us anymore. The thing that hurt me the most was when my mother decided to send me with my father, so I did not remind her of him! My father did not want me to join him because he could not care for me alone. Therefore, he came up with the idea to send me to his mother's house. That was the last time I saw or heard from my mother.

My grandmother lived in Sicily, Italy. I could tell she was kind but set in her ways. I did not know much about her, but she seemed excited to have me. My dad pulled up to the house and greeted my grandmother. They both conversed in Italian. I did not understand them at all. The conversation had come to an end. He then kissed me on the forehead and walked out of her house. That was the last memory I had of my father. He vanished from my life as if he never existed. Why would my father and mother do me that way? Was it my fault for their divorce? It seemed like I was the blame. My heart was so empty. I was so lost for words. I felt helpless. Who gave them the right to disown me that way? Just like that, they were out of my life. They gave up on each other, and they gave up on me. Then my dad decides to leave me with a stranger?

I was nervous, and I wondered if it was because I was only five years old. I felt all alone. My grandmother tried to make the best of it and welcome me as best she could. Her name was Lily, just like mine. Now I knew where my name derived. Lily stands for confidence, pride, and wealth. Grandma was all those things and more from the looks of it. I was so amazed by the beauty of her home. She was rich with class. Nothing looked cheap. Therefore, I was cautious of what I touched or sat in her home. Grandma had plenty of money just from the looks of how she lived.

Her hair was as white as snow with one streak of black. She was so beautiful and stood out in a crowd, but I didn't want to be like her. I had my own style, and I was comfortable in it. I'm just a plain Jane kind of girl. I don't care too much for fancy things. I love long sundresses, flat sandals, a neckless, and a pair of small earrings—nothing over the top for me. I never really wanted to be noticed. My father would say, "you look like the sun that sits in the sky, and you are as beautiful as the lilies in my mother's garden." I knew I was different from other girls. To know that grandma and I shared the same name gave me a sense of closeness to her.

Grandma's name fit her well because her favorite flower was a lily. She had lots of pretty flowers all over her home, but most were yellow lilies. She loved her yellow lilies, equating them to thankfulness, desire, and enjoyment. I remember my dad would buy lilies sometimes. I guess they reminded him of his mother. He never really talked about her, and we never asked him why.

My new journey began, and I was unsure how I felt about it. Grandma Lily looked at me with a smirk on her face to say she had something in store for me. I did not know if it was good or bad, but I prayed it was good. Grandma Lily already had the finest school picked out for me. Her favorite words were, "my family has plenty of money. So, nothing is too expensive for us to have. If we want it, we get it." Then she would laugh. Grandma wanted me to enjoy the best things since I now stayed with her. Grandma had such a stern and loving heart, all wrapped up in one. She didn't play about education or the career path we chose. You better believe she stayed on me to ensure I was doing good.

We visited different places in Sicily. Although I knew grandma wanted the best for me, sometimes I believe she just enjoyed showing off her riches to the neighbors. We visit places on the Island of Sicily like the Mediterranean Sea, Mt. Etna, and Palermo. As a child, doing and learning so many great things was truly exciting for me. Life continued to move forward. I no longer wondered about the whereabouts of my mother and father. I did not bother my grandma about if they would come back for me either. I realized I had the best loving grandmother, which comforted me. My happiness was all that mattered to me. Life was pretty good.

The years had flown by super-fast. My grandmother was up in age. She always had help because she hired a maid and butler. They even traveled with her sometimes. The things she could do herself when I first met her, she could no longer do. She loved working in her garden, though. She would grow and pick the most delicious fruits and vegetables. Only grandma was allowed in the yard. She did not want anyone else tampering with her garden. After watching her, I had to ask her why not just buy the fruits and vegetables from the store? She replied, "it's just not the same when you grow your own foods. It's a different taste and texture altogether." Well, I guess that settled it. Fresh fruits and vegetables were best in her opinion. Grandma Lily had her way of doing things, so I didn't pass judgment. I was just grateful that she took great care of me.

The chapter of high school was just about complete. I had many ups and downs, but overall, it was good. Everything was set in motion for college, and I was excited. I looked forward to the summer because it was my last moment of being free to explore before the workload of college took over my schedule. I did not have any plans for summer, but I knew it would not be bland like all the rest. My friends and I were going to cut up, meet good-looking men, and have a wonderful time. Grandma Lily will not know too much about what I'll be doing because she will be taking a trip with her best friend. Grandma will load my credit card with money so that I won't lack anything. I will do some shopping, nothing fancy. I am not a big shopper, so the items will have to catch my eye. Overall, I am excited to hang out with my friends.

CHAPTER 2

Alonzo Is So Fine

Today is the last day of school, and the party is on for the summer! The pizzeria was the hot hang-out spot. I could not wait to get there because my best friends waited for me. They were Italian, but I understood their language very well. I was a quiet person but peculiar, not in a weird way. I just did things a little differently from other folks. Grandma Lily was packed and ready to leave for her trip. Excitement had overtaken me. Grandma trusted me to be responsible, and I knew I could handle it. The first thing on my list was to prepare for the evening of hanging out with my friends. I knew it was going to be a long night! I made sure I did my hair beautifully and neatly. I love my pretty silky hair that came from my mother and father. Thank God I have something nice to remember them. Others always compliment me on my hair. I took out my yellow and white sundress to wear. Most of my clothes are solid yellow or yellow and white. I love the color yellow. I guess that's what makes me peculiar, and I love it.

Time to shower and get dressed. 8:00 pm is the meet-up time, and I must be ready, so my best friend can pick me up. She drives a Mercedes Benz so that I will be riding in style. My phone rang, and it was my best friend stating she was outside. I raced down the steps and jumped in the car. I was ready for the time of my life. It's Friday, and I am feeling beautiful. Driving through the city at night is so breathtaking. The lights gleam off the houses, and the radiance that comes from the moon sets the perfect scenery. The moonlight seems to follow us as we drive, but we know the moon sits still. We are almost at the pizzerias to meet up with the other girls. Yes, they too have cars. I just need a little more time to handle that type of responsibility. I'm okay with walking or catching a ride. I get to ride around and have fun with Luna. She doesn't mind, then neither do I.

We finally made it to the pizzeria. Luna and I sat down with the other girls laughing and conversing. We had not hung out in a while. As we spoke, who walked in the door? Alonzo, that's who! I almost melted. I turned around and did not lock eyes with him as I wanted. I did not want to seem desperate. I had been watching him for some time. I just haven't dared to say anything. I was too nervous and shy, I guess. Luna knows him well because they met during childhood. So, hopefully, she will hook us up, and I won't have to say anything. Luna knows how much I like him because I talk about him so much. When he looks at me with his sexy brown eyes, I melt like a chocolate popsicle. He has silky curly hair like the noodles I love. Pasta dishes are my favorite. Let's not talk about that body of his, oh my! Let me stop. I'm drooling like hell just thinking about him. I daydream about him often. He was meeting up with his friends in the pizzeria as well. My eyes would not let him out of my sight, although I tried. A girl named Camilla liked him too. She was also there that night. She decided to approach Alonzo to strike up a conversation. I immediately grew pissed! The only way she would get him was over my dead body. I don't know if she knew I had a thing for him, or she was just being spiteful.

I know I'm not entirely Italian, but I am still from an Italian bloodline on my father's side. That should be good enough. As I went back and forward in my head about Camilla approaching Alonzo, he turned and stared at me. I froze! I turned to Luna, and she smiled at me. He started heading my way after blowing off Camilla. I guess he was not interested in her. Alonzo blew her off like a bug on the wall. He walked up to me and said, "Hi." My mouth was glued shut. I didn't know what to say. I oozed into a sweat. My hands felt clammy and cold. I felt a little sick. I froze! I was in my head telling myself to say hello, but it would not come out at that moment. I felt crazy, but I eventually got the words out of my mouth. I could not get past that sexy Italian accent he had. He said, "Hello. How are you?" My heart just melted to the floor. What was happening to me?

I did not expect to react this way. I planned on playing it cool, but I blew that. Thank God he did not look at me as a weirdo. Instead, he waited for me to respond. He then asked me what I liked to do for fun? He wanted to know if it was dancing or going on crazy adventures. I looked at him and smiled. He begged me to respond as if he was really interested in my answers. I finally got out the word, yes. I told him I didn't do much of anything, but I loved trying new things. So, he asked me out on a date, and I screamed in my head. I could not believe it was happening! I fantasized about this day for a while but could not get the answer out of my mouth. It seemed that he thought I was playing hard to get, so he answered for me. He told me he just had to see me again, so I nodded to agree. He walked away, and Luna gave me a thumbs up from across the room.

Alonzo and I started visiting different places together. It was magical. It was everything I ever dreamed of, but sometimes I felt I was not good enough to be with him. Why did he choose me? What did he see in me? I'm just a plain girl, no car, and no fancy clothes like the other girls. I was unique, but not everyone could appreciate that. If he were hiding anything, it would come out to the light. I prayed he was not hiding anything, and this relationship was genuine. Until then, I will just enjoy the moment. Alonzo liked to eat. He didn't care too much for fast food like the pizzeria. Alonzo only hung out there with his friends. He was not too much of a talker once we started hanging out. He loved to read books and study. Alonzo also talked about the universe a lot. I could care less about his interests, so I tried to change the topics often.

Saturday evening, we decided to go out to dinner. He had the loveliest place in mind to take me. Dining in Sicily was so phenomenal! The stars shined bright like diamonds, and the streetlights made the neighborhood look so peaceful. We went to a lovely restaurant called OSTERIA ANICA MARINA. It made my heart sing because I loved delicious seafood! That restaurant was known for its one-of-a-kind seafood entrees. How did he know? Could Luna have told him? Or did he just take a guess? Luna is the only one who knows a lot of details about me. I'll find out later when I meet up with the girls to talk. The ambiance of the restaurant was gorgeous. I've never been to a place like it before. Alonzo made reservations. Therefore, the waiter sat us at our table soon as we walked in the door. That was surprising coming from a teenager. I was so blown away. I could give him a few points for that.

The waiter gave us menus and waited to take our order. I looked over the menu, and everything sounded so delicious. Alonzo grabbed my hand and told me to order whatever I wanted because the night was all about me. He considered me his queen. It made me blush every time he called me queen. I was in heaven. I ordered lobster and a salad with grilled shrimps and muscles. It was nice to eat something else besides pizza. Alonzo ordered the same. That was strange because he never did that. I guess who cares, right? He was so sexy as I stared into his dreamy eyes.

He ordered a glass of red wine, but not for me. I didn't drink and never would. I didn't want to start any bad habits, and I already knew my Grandma Lily would kill me. She would always say, "stay away from the bad men and bad things." Therefore, I did. I don't think Alonzo is an evil man, but it's too early in our relationship to find out yet. We talked and laughed as we ate our dinner. I did not realize he was such a comedian. Listening to his silly jokes passed the time.

Dinner came to an end, and we were ready to go. He paid the bill with his fancy credit card, and off we went. I noticed he didn't tip the waiter, though. I felt a little bad because I knew their actual income was their tips, not their paycheck. We walked to his car. He opened the door like a respectable man, and I got in. Then he got in, started the car, and off he drove. Alonzo pulled up to my house, walked me to the front door, and kissed my hand. "Goodnight. I hope to see you tomorrow, my Lily," said Alonzo. I turned to him and said, "yes, we will meet again tomorrow, my love." I went into the house and closed the door. I was so tired that I did not even call my friends to have a girl talk. Lights out and in the bed, I fell to sleep.

Sunday morning, and I'm ready for our day together. I was still kind of tired from the night before. I thought the shower would refresh me, but it only helped a little. Not as much as I hoped, though. I wore my favorite yellow sundress. I hope Alonzo likes it, although I may need an upgrade. I just don't want to turn him off because I love the attention he's giving me now. I do want to do some shopping. Maybe Alonzo and I could go together. There was a knock at the door, and in came Alonzo. We were so excited to see each other. I could stare at him all day. Alonzo and I went out for breakfast. We went to an ordinary restaurant, nothing fancy this time. We pulled up, and he opened my car door. We entered the restaurant and placed an order. I ordered eggs and bacon. I wasn't hungry because I was still a little exhausted from the night before. Alonzo ordered eggs, bacon, and waffles. I guess he was hungry. When we were done eating, he paid the bill, and we left. We went to the mall to shop and hang out a little. We went to the Outlet Village, where they had some of everything for a reasonable price. My eyes lit up like a kid in a candy store. That outlet had all the latest fashion and products.

Alonzo saw how excited I was and told me he had me covered. He said, "my sweet Lily, buy yourself whatever you want. Money is no big thing to me. Change up your style a little. Try something new for me. Live a little today." He smiled at me as he chuckled. Well, I guess there is a first time for everything. Here I go into something new. I thought the jeans looked nice and the blouses were gorgeous. They also had dresses! I got six pairs of jeans, some blouses, and eight dresses. The shoes there were so beautiful. I matched a pair to every outfit I picked out. I couldn't believe the pocketbooks were even eye-catching. Alonzo did say I should get what I wanted, and money wasn't a problem, so I did. I was finally done, and Alonzo paid for everything. He took me back home because he had some business to handle. I thought it was kind of strange since it was a Sunday. But it was fine. I did get to eat breakfast and went shopping for new clothes with him. This break gave me some time to hang out with the girls. I decided to call Luna to catch up and show off my new clothes.

Luna answered the phone and was excited to hang out later at the pizzeria. I missed her. I had not seen her in a while since I started dating Alonzo. Luna asked if Camilla could hang out with us, and I told her I did not feel comfortable with her around. Luna respected my wishes and did not allow Camilla to join us. I just did not trust her ever since she pulled that stunt on Alonzo. I am sure she knew I liked him but tried to talk to him anyway. I don't like her for that. I keep getting this feeling that they know each other more than it seems. I'm sure it will reveal itself sooner or later if that is the case. I pray I am wrong, though, because I enjoy hanging out with Alonzo. Luna agreed to pick me up at 8:00 pm, which is the time everyone will be at the hangout spot. I took a nap and got up in time to shower and a bite to eat. I wore my new jeans, blouse, matching shoes, and purse. I felt like a new and improved person. Luna pulled up outside, blowing the horn. I ran down the steps and off to the spot we went.

The weather felt so good that night. We couldn't wait to make it to the pizzeria to have fun. We pulled up and walked in. Guess who was the first person that caught my eye. Alonzo! He was sitting with Camilla all hugged up as if they were together. They did not see me, nor did Alonzo expect me to show up. I thought I saw things, so I had to blink my eyes a few times before reacting. Nope, it was Alonzo and Camilla in the flesh. He leaned over and kissed her, smack dead on her mouth. Luna looked with such shock in her eyes.

I did as well. I ran over to the table where Alonzo was sitting and asked what was going on? "Alonzo, I thought you had something to take care of tonight.

I guess this was it," Lily yelled. "Camilla, I thought you were my friend. I would hate to see you as my enemy," Lily said as she wiped tears from her face. "I'm so disappointed in both of you. I never want to talk with either of you ever again," Lily told Alonzo and Camilla. Lily turned to Luna and asked her to take her home. Luna tried to comfort Lily, but nothing worked. Lily just held her head down and cried all the way home, not saying a word. Luna pulled up to her front door. Lily got out and ran into the house, slamming the door. Luna didn't hear from Lily for some time. About a month had passed. There were two months of summer left, and no one had heard from Lily.

CHAPTER 5

Romeo, Oh Romeo

It's mid-July already, and I haven't found it within myself to go outside after the breakup. The summer is not going as I would have liked it to go. I did not expect to experience a broken heart. That is not what I had in mind when I said I wanted to have fun. I guess I should have left Alonzo as a crush instead of making him my boyfriend. I have just been sitting here gazing out the window every day instead of going out with my friends. Each day I notice a beautiful sparrow is sitting outside my window on the branch. I never saw it before. The sun was bright and the sky blue as the ocean. The sparrow sits so peacefully and free. It doesn't look like it has a care in the world. If only I could get to this point in my life.

June is over, and so is my relationship, but I'm still hurting inside. Seeing Alonzo together with Camilla truly pains me. I do know time heals all wounds, so I pray this time of healing for me moves expeditiously. If only I could show them how much they hurt me. Maybe it's just for me to move on and not look back. I thought Luna was my friend as well. She said she had no clue what was going on. I just don't believe that. I don't know if I can trust anyone anymore! I think she knew and kept the secret because Camilla is her friend too. Camilla and Alonzo seemed very close as if they had known each other for some time. I can't understand why he would even talk to me if he were only going to choose Camilla. I am sure Alonzo knew he would get caught because we all hung out at the same spot, and she was supposed to be my friend. It was almost as if he set me up to look like a fool. I'm over it now and ready to start a new life with new connections.

I remembered my grandma Lily saying to stay away from bad people and bad things. I should have recognized the signs. I was so caught up in his looks and the fact that she called me friend. I must forgive myself for falling into the trap of connecting with bad people. I must get out of this house. I have been shut in the house for almost a whole month. Love hurts when it's not the love you expect to receive. As I think back over my life, I thought I was over my mother and father disowned me. Alonzo only ripped the bandage off the wound I thought was healed. First, my mother and father did not want me, and now Alonzo? He doesn't want me either. Will anyone ever want me? I have a feeling no one will at the rate I'm going. What have I done so wrong for people I love to walk away? I was so lost and desperately wanted real love. Okay, let me pull myself together. I am standing here talking to myself for too long. I think I will shower and go for a walk. It's so beautiful today. Alonzo brought me new clothes, but I haven't worn anything since we broke up. I might as well wear them and enjoy the rest of my summer alone or until I meet someone new.

As I stepped out of the house, it felt like a new neighborhood. The weather was perfect, not too hot but just right. I saw the neighbors planting in their garden. They were enjoying the fresh air and laughing with one another. The question is, when did they start a garden? That is something Grandma Lily would do if she were back from her vacation. I missed her very much. I wish she were here to encourage me. Sometimes you just need a loyal person to allow you to vent to them or cry on their shoulder. I needed to hear, "it was going to be ok." I guess I will have to encourage myself in the meantime.

The neighbors waved at me. I waved back and kept going. Walking actually felt great. I have missed a lot of fresh air since I was shut up in the house all that time. It was getting late; therefore, I started heading back to the house. While walking, I noticed a black Toyota Corolla following me for quite some time. When I arrived home, the car slowed down, and the window came down. I was a little nervous and looked around to see if anyone else was out. I heard a sweet sexy voice echo from the car saying, "Hello, how are you?" I was hesitant to answer because I knew not to talk to strangers. I finally answered, "Hello, I'm great!" Then I proceeded to walk up the steps. As I glanced back, a guy with the face of an angel stuck his head out of the window. He was beyond handsome. He was dreamy! He asked if he could have a word with me, and I decided to give him a moment of my time. "My name is Romeo," he said. Therefore, I told him my name. He asked if he could have my number to chat with me later. I figured it was ok since I was single and was not rushing into anything else. Having someone to converse with in my free time seemed harmless. I gave him my number, and then I went into the house. I was a little exhausted, so I took a nap.

I woke up around 9 pm and checked my phone, hoping I did not miss the call from Romeo. To my surprise, there was no missed call. Maybe he is busy. I guess I will get something to eat. There was only cold chicken in the refrigerator. I did not want to order anything, so I just warmed up the chicken to eat. I rechecked my phone, and no Romeo. Maybe he forgot that he was supposed to call me tonight. I will just watch some television to pass the time. Hopefully, Romeo calls before I go to bed. I didn't want to call him first. I was not trying to seem desperate, nor did I want to experience a broken heart again. I tried to keep myself as occupied as I could to silence my thoughts of pain.

In my alone time, I found myself missing my parents. I was tired of fighting the hurt of abandonment. I did not want to pretend for everyone or lie to myself anymore. The pain and damage started a cycle of low self-esteem, worthlessness, and self-sabotage in my life. That is why I am interested in the guys that are no good for me. They manipulate me, find my soft spot, then deceive me. I don't see their real intentions until it is too late because I am desperate for love. Love is all I can think of these days. I wish I could focus on something else, but I can't.

Maybe that's why I desire a relationship so bad, although I do not want the hurt. I just want someone trustworthy. I remember how my father treated me as if I was his world. I enjoyed that, and I miss it dearly. He used to compliment me regularly and take me out. I knew he loved me until he gave me away. Now, I am unsure what love is because I do not think it will give someone special away. That love hurts. I even received that same love from other people, including Alonzo. I just want to find genuine love. I know it's out there. I will not give up on love. Will I receive it from Romeo? I pray it's him. I hope he calls soon so I can get to know him. I am a little shocked he did not call me yet since he followed me all the way home like a crazy stalker. I will sit and read one of Grandma Lily's books to relax since there is nothing else on television.

It's late, and still no Romeo. Could he be waiting for me to call him? I am a little anxious, but I am not calling him first! Nope! No way! Oh well, I guess he forgot, or maybe he has a girlfriend already. One will never know. I'm going to turn in for bed now. I do not want to wait any longer. I'm getting tired of the people who play games with my emotions, though. Tomorrow is a new day, so I will see what it may bring. As the sun rises, my alarm clock goes off, and I stretch as I turn it off. It's such a beautiful Tuesday morning today. It could not have come fast enough for me. The sun is bright, and the air is fresh. I'll shower and get dressed early, then go on my walk. Maybe I'll run into Romeo.

Lily began singing to herself as she started her morning routine. Lily made a piece of toast and a glass of orange juice for breakfast, then off to her walk. She took her cell phone just in case Romeo called. She didn't want to miss his call. "Lord, please let him call soon," Lily prayed. As Lily started her walk, she noticed the neighbors were outside. Lily stopped for a short moment to observe them showing love to one another. It was sweet to watch. They were always in a cheerful mood.

Lily yelled to the neighbors, "Good morning." They waved at her and smiled. Lily's phone began to ring. Guess who it was, Romeo, that's who! Lily was so excited that she almost dropped her phone trying to answer. Anxiety came over Lily as she said Hello. She knew she needed to calm down before Romeo could hear her breathing heavy. Lily counted to ten in her head, and to her surprise, it helped. "Hello, Romeo," Lily said. "Hi, Lily," replied Romeo. "I'm happy to hear your voice, Lily. Thank you for answering my call," expressed Romeo. Lily had to play it cool even though she wanted to ask him why he didn't call the night before. Lily responded, "No problem, Romeo. It is nice to hear your voice too!" Romeo asked, "What are you up to?" "I am out for a walk on this lovely day," said Lily. "Can I see you tonight? I would like to take you out to a delicious dinner named DA Vittorio. It's such a lovely, luscious place. I promise you will enjoy every bit, Lily," Romeo explained. Lily replied, "Well, since you put it like that, yes. Is 9:00 pm good for you, Romeo?" "Yes, Lily, that's good timing. I will pick you up at nine. I'll talk to you later. Have an amazing day. Bye, Lily," responded Romeo. "Bye Romeo," replied Lily. Lily was so happy. She pleaded with God to make Romeo the one she had been looking for all this time.

Summer will be over soon, and Lily wanted to experience a good man in her life before leaving for college. Lily was over bad men. She wanted a change, and Romeo was waiting to give her that. Lily returned to the house to pick out something nice to wear for her date. She could not believe she was going out again after Alonzo broke her heart. Lily was excited and could not wait for Romeo to arrive. She decided to take a nap after showering and laying out her clothes. Lily wanted to be well-rested so she could stay out as long as needed. It was 8:15 pm, and Lily's alarm clock went off. She did not want to be late for her date. Her mother used to push her to be on time because it was important. Lily's mother would jokingly say, "I pray you do not be late to your own funeral." "Those were the good days," Lily thought to herself.

Lily put on her yellow and white dress and white sandals. She pinned up her hair then waited for her handsome prince to arrive. "Oh, he is so sexy. I'll sit waiting by the front window," thought Lily. She tried to be patient, but the excitement overtook her. Lily started pacing back and forward at the window until she saw headlights. It was Romeo pulling up to the house. She did not want to seem desperate, so she waited until he blew the horn. Romeo honked the horn, and Lily ran down the stairs to the door.

Lily spoke to Romeo as she got into the car, "Hello, Romeo. How are you?" "Hello, Lily, my love! You're as beautiful as the sunset God created," Romeo replied. "Thank you, Romeo. You are so kind with words," said Lily. We pulled off to start the night. The restaurant we pulled up to was fabulous! Da Vittorio was known for their spaghetti. Everyone seems to brag about it, so I figured I would give it a shot. I ordered spaghetti and a salad, and Romeo ordered spaghetti and a glass of white wine.

Romeo turned to Lily as he signed for the waiter to return to their table, "Oh, Lily. Forgive me. Where are my manners? Would you like a glass of wine as well?" "No, thank you," said Lily. They began to talk. Romeo asked questions about Lily's five-year plan? He wanted to know if she planned to travel. What career she had in mind? What did she want to accomplish? Lily had no clue. She had no five-year vision or plan for her life other than finding a man and going to college. The date became weird. Lily felt Romeo was well educated because he asked out-of-the-box questions. She felt small-minded and stupid when she could not produce any of the answers for him. Romeo saw how uncomfortable Lily got, so he asked her if she wanted to dance. Lily assumed that was his way of changing the subject and breaking the ice. Lily was done with questions anyway. They danced until they were tired. Romeo paid for the tab, and they left the restaurant. Romeo pulled up to Lily's house and walked her to the door. He kissed Lily on the cheek and told her he would call the next day. Lily told him good night and went to bed.

It's Wednesday morning, and Lily is up early but tired. She hoped for something new and exciting to happen because Wednesdays are such a drag for her with nothing to do. Lily sat around waiting for Romeo's call. "I hope Romeo calls. We had such a great time at the start of our date until he asked me many questions. I pray Romeo did not lose interest in me. He did end the date rather quickly," Lily thought to herself. Lily started her morning off by grooming herself, and then she heard her phone ring.

"Oh, my! Let me hurry up and answer the phone. It could be Romeo," Lily thought. Lily answered the phone, "Hello, who's calling?" Romeo replied, "Hello, my sweet Lily. How are you this beautiful morning?" Lily responded, "I'm great! What will we be doing this evening?" Romeo answered, "Lily, my love, I would love to go see a movie at the MULTICINEMA THEATHER. I heard it's really nice there. Would you like to go? If so, what time is good for you? Eight or nine tonight will work for me. We can pick out a movie when we arrive there. That's the fun of it all." "Well, Romeo, I guess 9:00 pm would be good," said Lily. "I will see you then, Lily," Romeo replied.

Lily finished showering and made herself an omelet with a hot cup of tea. She decided to turn her phone off for the rest of the day. She wanted no distractions from anyone. "I guess I'll take out a pair of jeans, a lovely blouse, and my gorgeous Gucci bag for tonight. I want to look beautiful for my new man. Oh, did I say my man? I guess I did," Lily smiled to herself. "I pray this guy is the one for me, Lord. Romeo seems to be so respectful, and he's such a gentleman," Lily prayed. Lily nodded off as she meditated on the thought of Romeo. Time flew by, and it was 8:00 pm. Lily jumped up and rushed to see what time it was and realized she still had a little time to get ready. "This night should be fun. Romeo appears to be such a great guy. I can't say too much for the last man I dated. He turned out to be a mess. He was a liar and not a good one at that. Well, no more talk about my past relationship," Lily said to herself.

It was nine o'clock, and Romeo pulled up on time to pick Lily up for their date. Lily was so excited that she made her way outside in no time. Lily greeted Romeo, "Hello, Romeo. How are you this lovely evening?" Romeo replied, "Hello, Lily. I'm better now that I see you. Are you ready to go?" "Yes, I'm ready," said Lily with great excitement. They then proceeded to the theater. The moon was so beautiful, the sky was clear, and the stars sparkled brightly as diamonds. They soon arrived at a huge, extravagant theater. Lily was blown away because she had never seen anything like it. This theater did not compare to any other theater she had ever seen. Romeo purchased the tickets and scanned the food menu to see what he wanted to buy. He ordered hot dogs, popcorn, and soda pops for them both. The door ushers took Romeo and Lily to their seats, and the movie began.

Romeo chose a horror film, but Lily did not like scary movies. Lily remained quiet the whole time as she buried her face in her hands for every suspense scene. Romeo asked Lily if she was ok when he noticed Lily was not watching the movie. Lily expressed she was afraid of the movie. Romeo began to laugh at Lily because he found her fear amusing. Lily tried to cover up that she was frightened after Romeo laughed at her. "I was joking. Nothing is wrong. I'm just a little distracted from watching the movie. I'm thinking about you, that's all," Lily replied, brushing Romeo off. Lily's heart was racing, and her hands were sweaty. She wanted to leave but did not know how to tell Romeo. She did not want to mess up the date as she felt she did the previous night. Romeo insisted that she tell him what was wrong. Lily told him she did not like scary movies, and Romeo laughed harder. Lily figured if she went to the restroom, it would help her get away without causing a scene. She turned to Romeo and told him she would be back after using the restroom. He asked her to hurry back so she didn't miss the movie, not knowing that was Lily's plan altogether.

When Lily went into the ladies' room, she spotted one of her girlfriends she hadn't seen in a while. "Hello, Bettina. How are you? We haven't seen each other for some time," said Lily. Bettina replied with a smile, "yes, Lily. We haven't. You look so amazing. How is everything?" Lily responded, "Thank you so much! Everything is just great. I have a new man in my life, and I'm really excited. The wonderful thing about this relationship is that he's all mine. Would you like to meet him?" "Yes, that would be nice only if you're ok with me meeting him, Lily," said Bettina as she remembered the scene with Alonzo. "Don't be silly. I don't mind at all," expressed Lily. Bettina and Lily walked out of the restroom to meet up with Romeo. Lily got Romeo's attention and introduced him to Bettina. It seemed like another awkward moment for Lily, as if Romeo and Bettina knew each other. Romeo greeted Bettina, and she immediately had an urgency about leaving. "It was nice meeting you," Bettina said to Romeo as she grabbed Lily to walk her to the door.

"I hope you both are thrilled to be together," continued Bettina as she hugged Lily and walked off. "That was strange," Lily thought to herself. Before Lily could make it back to Romeo, he met her at the door and was ready to leave. Lily did not understand why Romeo was in a hurry to go also, and he chose the movie for them to see. As Romeo started up the car, he asked Lily if she was hungry to lighten the mood. "No, I am not hungry. I would like to call it a night, if you don't mind," Lily expressed. "No problem, my love. Anything for you," said Romeo. Lily started to get that feeling inside that something was wrong but didn't want to jump to conclusions. Romeo drove Lily home, walked her to my door, then kissed her good night. She went into the house, turned off her phone, and just wanted to sleep.

It's daybreak, and Lily is ready for a fresh start. She went out on her daily walk thinking about her movie date. Lily still had a strange feeling about Romeo and Bettina. It gave her flashbacks of Alonzo and Camilla. Lily prayed she was not in a repeat situation. She trusts Bettina, but the feeling would not go away. By the time Lily got back home, her phone had rung. Lily answered the phone, "Hello. Who's calling?" "It's me, Bettina. How are you? Are you free? I need to talk to you," Bettina said. Lily replied, "I'm fine. How about you, Bettina? What is going on?" Bettina responded, "I'm great. It was terrific seeing you last night. Look, Lily. I'm not going to beat around the bush. How long have you known Romeo?" "A month. Why? What's going on? Please, answer," said Lily feeling concerned. Bettina got quiet and asked Lily to sit down for the news. Lily immediately got upset. "Look, Bettina. If you have something to say, just say it! I don't have time for games," said Lily. Bettina blurted out, "Romeo's married! Didn't you know?" "How would I have known anything like that? He's been taking me out to beautiful places and treating me like a queen. So, no, I didn't know. Why would he lie about something like that? I've fallen in love with Romeo, and I know in my heart that he loves me too," replied Lily with frustration.

Lily went quiet for a second and thought about it. It explained a lot of Lily's questions. It made perfect sense! Lily screamed, "I'm so stupid. How could I be so blind not to see this? Maybe that's why he always wanted to only take me out at night. Wow, this is so unbelievable! Why would he want to hurt me like that? Thank you, Bettina. I appreciate your honesty." "You're welcome, Lily. I'm so sorry you had to hear this. I know you are hurting right now, Lily, but you must let him go. Tell Romeo that you found out he's married. He's been married for five years now and has two kids. What he is doing to you and his family is so wrong. He is living a lie," expressed Bettina. "Yea, it's wrong, and I am angry right now! Let me go. I must get my mind right after what I just heard. I'll call you later. Goodbye, Bettina," Lily disappointedly replied.

Lily was so upset. She knew something was strange, but never would have guessed Romeo was married! She called Romeo, and he picked up on the first ring. "Hey, Lily, my love. How are you on this lovely day? I miss you," said Romeo. "I'm not good at all. My heart is broken. I need to ask you a question, and I want you to be honest," explained Lily. "Yes, my Lily. What is it? I will answer whatever you ask," replied Romeo. "Are you married? Do you have two children? I need the truth, please. I have fallen in love with you, and I thought you felt the same for me, Romeo," Lily cried. "Lily, I don't know what to say," Romeo responded. "Just tell me the truth. Don't you think I deserve that, Romeo? I thought I knew you," expressed Lily. "Yes, I am married, Lily. The first time I saw you, I just couldn't help myself. I love you, my sweet Lily! I don't know how it is possible, but I do. Do you believe that? I pray you see my heart," Romeo pleaded with Lily. "No, I do not believe anything you say now, and I hate you for lying to me. I have been through so much pain with men, and you are no different. I trusted you, and you took advantage of me. I pray your wife and kids find out what a jerk you are. I never want to see you ever again! Goodbye, liar," Lily yelled as she hung up her phone. Lily threw the phone on her dresser and laid across the bed with tears flowing from her eyes.

Lily started crying out to God. "Why does this always happen to me? Please, God. Tell me why? That was not fair," Lily prayed as she cried herself to sleep.

CHAPTER 4

Lorenzo, My Everything

The month of July has ended, and it's August 1ˢᵗ. Lily is hurt and all alone again! "I have nothing to do and no one to love me. I miss my Grandma Lily. This summer has not been good for me at all. After the last day of school, I thought I would have so much fun. It turns out I only explored darkness and brokenness," Lily thought to herself in disappointment. "God, I remember asking You why I kept getting hurt? What is wrong with me? Please answer me, Lord," pleaded Lily.

She noticed Grandma Lily's bible on the dining room table. It immediately sparked her interest, and she began to read *"Isaiah 41:10, "Do not fear for I am with you; do not be dismayed, for I am your God. I will strengthen you and help you; I will uphold you with my righteous right hand."* Lily remembered her mother and father reading this scripture whenever they felt things weren't going well. "Why didn't they remember the scripture when they grew apart? I wonder why they didn't get help. If they did, I would still be with them both," thought Lily.

Rejection and abandonment started speaking even louder to Lily. "No one wants me. I am never going to be with another man. I just can't take any more hurt or the lies. Well, God, you seemed to have failed my mother and father. I guess that's why you have failed me too! You never gave me the answer I was hoping to find. Talking to you feels pointless because you never reply with anything. Am I wasting my time seeking you for answers? I just thought answers were what you are known for," Lily shouted in anger to God. Lily gave up on talking to God at that moment and started her morning routine. She showered, brushed her teeth, and sang to herself for comfort. In no time, Lily was done grooming and off to the kitchen for breakfast. She made bacon, eggs, and a piece of toast. After eating, Lily decided to take a walk for some fresh air. She knew sitting in the house was unhealthy because she would go crazy with her thoughts.

"That's it! I'll go down to the pizza shop tonight. Everyone will be out enjoying themselves. Maybe I'll see Luna and Bettina there too," thought Lily as she walked the route she regularly took.

"That settles it. I have a date with myself this evening, and I'm ok with that," Lily laughed to herself. "Things will one day get better for me. At least, I hope they will," said Lily trying to encourage herself. Lily is done with her walk. She headed back home to relax and read a book. Once Lily got home, she began giggling to herself, saying, "maybe I'll read the bible to try getting answers from God that way. Who knows, it just might work." As Lily begins to read, she nods off.

It is 6:00 pm. Lily has woken from her nap. "Oh, my! I must have been exhausted. I can't believe it's six o'clock in the evening. Let me get myself together for my date night with myself. This will be a night to remember because it's me, myself, and I. Therefore, I don't have to experience any more disappointment that catches me by surprise," Lily said to herself while standing in the mirror. Lily got dressed and glanced at the clock to see that it was 8:00 pm already. Off to the pizzeria, she went.

Lily walked through the doors and saw Luna sitting at the table. "Hey, Luna! How have you been? It's been a while," said Lily. "Hello, Lily. I'm great. How are you? I did not expect to see you here tonight," replied Luna. "I'm good. I had another bad breakup, but other than that, I'm good. I want to apologize for being so nasty to you. It wasn't your fault about how things went down between Alonzo and me I. Alonzo was just a liar and made his own choice to hurt me. I hope we can still be friends," expressed Lily from a sincere heart. "Yes, I never stopped being your friend. I realized you were hurt, and I chose to be understanding. I missed you, Lily! I'm so glad you showed up here tonight. Let's grab something to eat," replied Luna as she wrapped her arms around Lily. "Great! Let's catch up. I missed you too, Luna," Lily responded with excitement. Lily and Luna then ordered pizza and soda pops. They began to reminisce and laugh about old stories and how the summer was not what they expected so far. Lily scanned the room to get a feel of who was there, and just like that, there she saw him. Lily's focus drifted away from the conversation she and Luna were having. Lily thought, "Who is he?"

A handsome man was sitting across from Lily and Luna. He had amazing eyes and skin like gold. His body built was so sickening! Just like that, Lily was in love again. "I must get to know him," Lily smiled to herself. Luna noticed Lily had drifted off. "Hey, girl! Are you listening to me? What is going on? I was talking to you," Luna yelled quietly while looking into Lily's eyes. "Girl, I'll tell you what is going on! See that guy over at the table across from us? Not that one, but him," Lily explained. "Yes, Lily. I can see him.

That's Lorenzo. He's single, I think. I never see him with anybody. He's always by himself. Please don't jump into a relationship too fast. Find out about him first. Lily, you sometimes move too fast, and that's not good. As your friend, do some research on his background first, please, Lily," responded Luna. "Alright, Luna. You are so scary at times. I got this. Don't worry about me, girl. I'll be just fine. Sometimes you must live a little," said Lily as she cleaned off the table.

Lily got up to put her trash in the recycle bin to try and get Lorenzo's attention. He noticed her beautiful walk and gorgeous hair. Therefore, he spoke. "Hello, dear. How are you? What is your name? You are beautiful," said Lorenzo. "Hi, my name is Lily. What's your name? Thank you for the compliment," expressed Lily. "My name is Lorenzo. Would you like to sit and talk? I would love your company," pleaded Lorenzo. "No, thank you. We can exchange phone numbers if that's ok with you. I am here with my friend, Luna, right now," Lily replied. Lorenzo said, "yes, that's fine with me. Can I call you sometime tomorrow, Lily?" Lily answered, "yes, that's great! I'll be waiting for your call. Have a good night." Lily and Luna then departed from the pizzeria and went their separate ways. Lily made it home, showered, and prayed before going to bed. She prayed and asked God to, please let Lorenzo be the right man for her. Lily wanted to take him as the future husband she desired to marry.

The next day Lily got up, and she heard some noise downstairs. She got nervous because she knew her grandma was still away. Therefore, no one should be in the house. Lily got up out of bed and grabbed a stick she saw in the corner by her bed. She opened the door and started down the steps really slow. Lily began to tremble a little because she was afraid of the unknown. She didn't want the person or persons to know she was on to them. Therefore, she had to act quickly.

Lily asked, "who's down there?" No one answered. "Hello, I'm going to ask again! Who is in my house? I am calling the police," Lily said as she tip-toed around the corner, ready to strike anyone there. A soft voice came out of the kitchen and said, "it's me, Lily, your grandma." Lily dropped the stick and ran to the kitchen. She grabbed her Grandma Lily and gave her the biggest kiss she could ever give. "Grandma Lily, why are you back so early?

Did something happen? You still have a couple of weeks of vacation left," Lily said. "I'd begun to miss you. I noticed you weren't calling or writing me. I needed to make sure everything was ok and to see for myself. I've been feeling something wrong with you. Would you like to sit and talk about your summer? I want to hear everything that's been going on," explained Grandma Lily.

"After I shower and eat breakfast if that's ok," replied Lily. "Ok, I will make breakfast and wait until you get yourself together. Lily, it looks like you haven't been eating at all. You look like you have been stressed out. I pray if you are stressed, it has nothing to do with your mother and father. I will say this, they both love you. You just have to start loving yourself first and live your life to the fullest. Enjoy life, but not in a foolish way. Seek the peace, love, and joy of God," said Grandma Lily trying to share wisdom with Lily. "Yes, Grandma Lily. I hear you. I'll be back down for breakfast in a minute," Lily responded as she walked away. Lily went upstairs to shower and get dressed. She made her bed up and gathered her thoughts to speak to Grandma Lily. She did not know what to share or what to keep to herself. Lily was done getting herself together and proceeded to the kitchen, where Grandma Lily awaited her arrival. Lily wondered if her grandma knew about anything in particular.

Grandma Lily started setting the table once she heard Lily walking down the steps. Grandma Lily then sat their breakfast on the table. Lily was a little nervous because she didn't have a clue what her grandma knew. She wondered if her grandma knew about the boyfriends she had or the guy she was dating. Grandma Lily asked, "what has been going on, Lily? The Lord has been dropping some things in my spirit that is not good." The weight on Lily's shoulders was so great. She wanted to keep everything to herself but knew it would eventually seep out at some point. Lily figured it was best to release it before her problems grew out of control. Lily opened up and began to share everything that had been going on since Grandma Lily was away. Lily even shared her breakups after trying to hold them in. She broke down and began to cry as she shared.

Lily asked, "why won't anyone love me, grandma? Many people have hurt me. They pretend to love me and then mistreat me. What am I doing so wrong?

First, my parents, then the last two relationships, and now I wonder about the guy I am currently dating. Is this my life? Why does God keep allowing these things to happen to me? I deserve love, too, right? Grandma explained, "It's not God's fault for the things we choose to do and the people we accept in our lives. We refuse to go to God for anything anymore, and then we want to blame Him for our shortcomings. So, when we make moves on our own, it falls on us, not God. Hurt, distrust, stealing, murder, sabotage, etc., happens when we don't want to accept Christ Jesus. We have to live a certain way and allow God to help us." "Well, Grandma Lily, I'm done talking for now. Can we talk tomorrow if that's ok with you? I have something to do today, and I don't want to miss out on it," interrupted Lily. Grandma Lily replied, "yes, but Lily, my sweet granddaughter, be careful with the decisions you make going forward. I'm talking from experience. The snakes you are dealing with keep biting. It's not the bite that kills; it's the venom. The snakes leave venom inside that contaminates and take over their host. That's what takes you out if you don't have the antidote to drain out the poison. I love you, Lily."

Lily walked outside to answer a phone call. It was Lorenzo. He wanted to talk to Lily about plans for their date. Lily replied, "Hey, dear. How are you? Lorenzo responded, "I'm great, Lily, my beauty. "What will we be doing today? I am excited to get out of the house. My grandma and I had a conversation this morning about life. She started talking about the Lord, and I wasn't ready for all that. It is still on my mind, though. I just want to go somewhere to unwind and enjoy myself," Lily shared as she stared at the beautiful colors in the sky. Lorenzo replied, "yes, Lily. I know how you feel. I'm still at work right now, so I must call you back. I can't wait to see you for a date tonight.

Lily was filled with joy for a date and asked, "sounds good! What time should I be ready?" "Around nine o'clock will give me enough time. I want to make sure I look good for a beautiful woman like you, Lily," Lorenzo explained. They both hung up from the call, and Lily went back into the house to her room. Grandma Lily noticed how Lily was avoiding her, but she paid it no mind. She just sat there in her rocking chair, not saying a word. Lily came back downstairs. "Oh, grandma. I didn't see you sitting there," said Lily. Grandma Lily just looked up at her, still saying nothing. Lily said, "grandma, I have a date tonight. I'll be leaving out at nine o'clock." Do what you must,

Lily," Grandma Lily said sarcastically. "Remember you have to make a choice in life, or you are setting yourself up for failure. Stop walking into the hurt. You will one day understand what I just said. You know I was once young too! I played some dangerous games as well. To heal from hurt, you must forgive yourself and the others who have hurt you," Grandma Lily continued as she rocked back and forward.

Lily asked, "Why would I have to forgive myself? I'm not the one hurting people. I do not understand." Grandma Lily replied, "You must begin forgiving yourself because you keep accepting the same hurt from different people, and that is what's weighing you down. Forgive yourself first, and then it will become easy to forgive others. Trust me, I know too well. I've been there before too many times to count. Talk with God concerning this process. I know you don't want to hear anything about God. That's why you cut our talk short after I brought God up. The choice is yours. If you choose incorrectly, you will continue to chase your tail like a dog but never catch it! Stop going in circles and examine your heart today before it's too late. Give it all to God! Believe me, when I say the Lord will bring you through every step of the process. Enjoy your new date. I pray you get whatever it is you're looking for in this man. Think about it. If you didn't find love in the first two men, what makes you think this guy is "the right one"? He might even know the other two gentlemen. You never know in this town," said Grandma Lily.

Lily looked at her grandma and said, "Well, I must find out on my own. I love you, grandma. I'm going to take a nap until it is time for me to get dressed for my date." Grandma Lily let the conversation go and shook her head in disappointment. Lily headed up to her room and took a nap. Hours later, Lily finally woke up from her nap and realized she needed to get ready quickly for her date with Lorenzo. Grandma Lily was in her bedroom watching television, trying not to focus on her conversation with Lily from earlier. She saw Lily walk past her room to go into the bathroom, but she ignored her. Lily called out to her grandma once she felt the tension, "Grandma Lily, are you ok?" Grandma Lily held back her emotions and replied, "yes, I'm fine. Thanks for asking." "Ok, grandma. I will be leaving for my date soon," said Lily. Grandma Lily didn't say anything, although she did not want Lily to go on a date. Grandma Lily tried to understand that Lily was getting older and needed to find her way. Grandma Lily knew she had to get her emotions out of the way and just pray. Therefore, Grandma Lily went off into a quiet place and prayed, asking God to take control of it all.

Lily began to pace back and forth, waiting on Lorenzo. Moments later, she heard the sound of a car horn. She looked out the window, and it was Lorenzo. Lily could not wait to get down the steps! She moved so fast she forgot to tell Grandma Lily goodbye! Lily got into the car, and they drove off. Lily was so happy that Lorenzo arrived when he did because she knew her grandma wanted to have another conversation. She asked Lorenzo to fill her in about their date because she had no clue what they were doing. Lily thought maybe he wanted it to be a surprise.

Lily asked, "where are we going on this beautiful night, Lorenzo?" "Well, Lily, I decided to take you to a theme water park to release some of the stress you are going through. Let's have fun and forget about the cares of the world," replied Lorenzo. Lily turned and looked at Lorenzo with an overflow of appreciation in her eyes. She was filled with joy simply because he cared about her state of mind and peace. They made it to the water park, entered in, and waited in line to buy tickets. Lily told Lorenzo she had the money for her ticket. "Please let a man do what a man is supposed to do, which is pay your way. You are my date. Relax, my queen. I got this, my sweetie," said Lorenzo. Lily smiled and put her money away. They entered the water park and got on the Scary Monster ride. They were both nervous. Once the ride started, they began screaming while holding each other and laughing hysterically until the ride was over. Lily felt so connected, loved, and special while in Lorenzo's presence, although she was unsure about the dynamics of their relationship.

They both enjoyed the night riding the water rides, embracing each other, eating cotton candy, pizza, and soda pop. It was getting late and time to go home. They left the water park. Lorenzo pulled up to Lily's house, kissed her good night, and drove off. Lily went into the house and headed up to her room, trying to avoid her grandma. Little did she know, Grandma Lily was looking out her bedroom window as Lily got out of the car. Lily showered, turned her phone off, and started to pray. "Dear God, please let this be the right man for me. I don't want another snake bite," Lily laughed to herself. "I don't know what my grandma meant by the snake bite, but I'm not looking for any trouble or more pain. Well, that's all, God, good night," Lily prayed, and off to sleep, she went.

The following day, Lily is already up and downstairs eating breakfast. Grandma Lily is still upstairs. Well, at least, that's what Lily is thinking. Lily never checked on her grandma to see if she was up or wanted breakfast. Lily left the house, and who did she see working in the garden? Grandma Lily was there planting new seeds. Lily's face hit the ground in shock. She did not expect her grandma to be up so early and in the garden. Grandma Lily saw Lily and said, "Good morning to you. How are you doing on this beautiful morning?" Lily replied, "Good morning, grandma. I am fine. Thank you for asking. How are you?" "I'm ok. I am happy you got in safe last night. Where are you headed early this morning? I am surprised you are up and out so soon," expressed Grandma Lily. "Oh, nowhere in particular. I am just taking a walk," said Lily as she covered up the meeting with Lorenzo. Grandma Lily quickly replied, "A walk, Lily? If you say so. Tell your friend I said hello and to please pick you up from the house. I want to see who you leave with just in case I need to locate you. Besides, tell him your grandma said a real man picks up a lady at the front door."

"Yes, ma'am," said Lily as she walked off to start her walk. Grandma continued to water her flowers and vegetables. She even began to pray. "Lord, please show my granddaughter that this man is nothing but trouble, in Jesus Christ's name, Amen," prayed Grandma Lily. Lily met up with Lorenzo on her walk. She was so excited to see him. Lily jumped in his car, kissed him on the lips, and they drove off. Lily asked, "Where are we going on this beautiful day, baby?"

Lorenzo informed Lily they were going on a picnic in the park by the lake. Lily was excited to do something different. "What are we eating on the picnic? I am sure it's something yummy," said Lily. Lorenzo replied, "Juicy strawberries, watermelon, grapes, crackers, and cheese. I also brought white wine so we could celebrate, my sweetie." Lily looked at Lorenzo and was hesitant to be upfront with him about wine. On second thought, she figured how hard could it be to open up to him? "I don't drink alcohol, and you shouldn't either. I'm not trying to be bossy. Do what you like, but I don't drink," Lily boldly responded as she hid her fear. "Ok, my Lily. You don't have to drink. I'll drink for the both of us. I do have some fresh spring water if you like. Lily took the spring water, and Lorenzo gave her a funny look. It seemed like he was upset with Lily because she turned down the wine. Lily felt the shift in his attitude. "Are you upset with me because I chose not to drink? I hope you are not," Lily asked. Lorenzo replied, "no, I just thought we would eat, drink, and relax so you could get comfortable. There is nobody here, and we could, you know, get a little loose. Do you know what I'm saying, Lily? I love you a lot and wanted to have you on another level." Lily was not excited about the date anymore. She wasn't looking for sex just yet.

They had only been dating for some weeks. Lily felt Lorenzo was moving too fast. "Please take me home. I think it is time for me to go now," Lily expressed as she walked towards the car. "Why? What is wrong? Did I offend you? I am sorry if I did," said Lorenzo. Lily replied, "nothing's wrong. I'm just ready to go." Lorenzo got angry with Lily because she shut down and chose not to say another word. "Ok, fine! I'll take you home," Lorenzo expressed, trying not to yell at Lily. They both got into the car, and neither of them said a word to each other the whole drive. Lorenzo dropped Lily off without a goodbye or a kiss. Lily went into the house and ran upstairs. She was not in the mood to have a conversation with anyone, especially her grandma. She wanted to be alone. Grandma Lily knew something was wrong but decided to say nothing. She did not want to get involved. The day went on in silence, and Lily slept the rest of the day away.

Lily woke up the next day and stayed in bed, hoping her phone would ring. She wanted Lorenzo to come to his senses and call. The evening fell, and he still had not called. Nevertheless, Lily tried not to care too much because the day was still young. Lily prayed, "Lord, why isn't Lorenzo calling me? I bet it's because I didn't want to drink. I know that's why he is upset. Men can be so dumb and inconsiderate. Lord, I'm not going to do anything to hurt my body. My parents didn't drink, and neither did my grandma. Therefore, I know I do not need it to enjoy myself. Maybe Lorenzo just doesn't want to be in a relationship anymore. Well, I'm not making the first move. He can call me to break it off if that's what he desires. Why do I trip out like this, Lord? Please make sense of it all."

Grandma Lily walked into Lily's room to ask her how her day was. Lily looked at her grandma with great disappointment and said, "I'm not having a good day. Lorenzo wanted me to drink white wine with him yesterday to get busy sexually. You do know what that is, grandma?" "Look here, Lily. You watch your mouth and show me some respect. Yes, I know just what that is, honey. How do you think your father was born? I pray you didn't do anything you will regret later. Do you understand what I'm saying? You know I love you with all my heart, Lily. Stop randomly picking and choosing what you think is good for you. Your flesh seems to have a hunger for bad men that lie and cheat on you. When are you going to start trusting God with your life? God has a plan and a purpose for you. Another thing, you weren't raised to act like some wild free beast. Get some control over yourself. You are falling for everything and ending up with nothing. Again, I love you, and remember, God loved you first and still does. I'm going out into my garden. Would you like to get dressed and help me? I promise it will relieve some of your stress," replied Grandma Lily. Lily said, "no, I don't feel like doing any gardening, grandma. You go and enjoy your alone time."

"Oh, I'm never by myself. My God is always here with me because He lives inside of me," responded Grandma Lily. Lily said with confusion, "I don't understand what you're saying." "If you gave your life to Jesus Christ, repented, turned from your evil ways, and asked for forgiveness, you shall be forgiven, Lily. Allow God to do great work in you and lead the way. Things will get a lot better; I guarantee. I want to let you know that there will still be challenges along the way. If you stay the course of reading The Word and applying it to your life, God will be on your side. Nothing will be impossible for God to fix or do in your life. Enjoy your day in bed, Lily. I have work to do," explained Grandma Lily.

Lily looked at her grandma with a puzzled look and laid back down. Grandma Lily went outside in her yard and began pulling up some vegetables. Lily continued to monitor her phone, and still no Lorenzo. The day quickly went by, and Lily remained in bed frustrated and sobbing. She did not even get out of the bed to wash, brush her teeth, or eat. Lily was depressed and broken-hearted because she knew her relationship was over with Lorenzo so soon. She thought he was "the one!" Lorenzo just turned out to be another one that broke her heart and wasted her time.

A couple of days went by, and Lily considered making plans for her day. She decided to get washed and dressed for the day too. Grandma Lily was downstairs cooking breakfast for the both of them. She was determined to get Lily out of bed. When Lily got downstairs to the kitchen, Grandma Lily was surprised to see her. "Good morning, grandma," Lily said. Grandma Lily replied in excitement, "Hello, Lily. How are you feeling this morning? I missed you walking around the house. I am glad to see you!" "Well, grandma, I'm still not doing too good. "What is wrong with me? Why does God keep allowing these things to happen in my life? I just want to be loved and understood, that's all," said Lily as she began to cry, trying not to scream. She was hurting inside. A broken heart is nothing to play with, ever.

Grandma Lily went over to the table where Lily had her head down crying and began to pray over her. After she was done praying, she kissed Lily on the forehead and said to her, "you must give God your life and desires. God loves you and wants the best for you, but the journey is up to you. God gives us "free will" to make our own choices. We can choose His plans for our lives or choose the popular things of this world. Sure, the world looks glittery and fabulous, but that's not all it's cracked up to be because the world goes against God's Will for our life," explained Grandma Lily.

Lily wiped her eyes and began to eat. She did not respond to anything Grandma Lily said because it was still processing in her mind. Grandma Lily left the situation alone and began to eat once she saw Lily shut down to herself. Lily's cell phone rang, and it was Lorenzo. Lily wondered if she should have answered. She picked up, figuring it was the right thing to do in case something terrible happened to prevent Lorenzo from calling her the previous days.

Lily decided to answer the phone. "Hello," she said. Lorenzo quickly cut her off, saying, "Hello, Lily. I am sorry, but I can no longer do this. I am moving on with my life, and I do not want to string you along anymore. Our relationship is over. I hope you find what you are looking for soon." Lily started to cry and ask, "Why? Please don't do this to me. What did I do to deserve this? Was it all because I did not want the wine? Or was it because I did not want to have sex with you right now? I love you, and this is how you treat me?" Lorenzo said, "Please don't cry. You're just not the woman I thought you were. You're too boring—no disrespect to you. I need a woman that's not afraid to do what I expect her to do, nothing personal. Yes, I wanted us to drink, have sex, and do whatever else I could think of, but you turned me down. I understand that is just not who you are, so I can't be with you anymore."

Lily hung up the phone while Lorenzo was still talking. She couldn't handle the mean things he was saying to her. Lily continued to cry. Grandma Lily grabbed Lily and held her, rocking her in her arms. Lily felt helpless, but her grandma assured her that everything would get better. Lily looked at Grandma Lily and said, "I truly hope things get better fast, grandma. I am hurt bad." Grandma Lily wiped Lily's tears away and replied, "He did you a favor by letting you go. You will understand all of this one day." Lily smiled, went up to her room, and stayed there all day to clear her mind.

CHAPTER 5

He Loves ME, HE Really Does!

Morning arrived, and Lily was awake but decided to stay in her room. Grandma Lily knocked on her door to check on her. She asked, "Are you ok, Lily?" Lily said with a sad voice, "No, I'm so tired of living! What's the point? Why did God create me? Was it just to go through all this hurt? Nobody wanted me, and the man I thought loved me just wanted sex. He wasn't even trying to marry me. Maybe if I had asked, he would have said "yes." That way, I would not have felt bad about sleeping with him." Grandma Lily looked at Lily and yelled, "child, are you crazy? That doesn't make things right! You would still be living a lie. You see how he treated you when he wanted to get you drunk and take advantage of you. Wake up, child, and get your life together. You might not like what I'm saying, but you need God to help you. The only way to do that is to give your life over to His Son, Jesus Christ." Lily asked, "how do you do these things you speak of grandma?"

Grandma Lily smiled and said, "baby, I'm glad you asked. According to Romans 10:9 NIV, "If you declare with your mouth, "Jesus is Lord," and believe in your heart that God raised him from the dead, you will be saved." "I will keep that in mind," Lily replied. "Is there a certain age I have to wait until or a special way to do it? I think I can at least declare and believe," said Lily.

Grandma Lily replied, "Don't make it difficult or confusing. Whatever the Word says to do, just do it. Remember, this is not about me. It is all about your relationship with God. It must be personal between you and the father, God. When we have a relationship with the Lord, we become one in spirit with him. That's the only way things will change. The Bible declares, according to Philippians 2:5-7 NIV, "In your relationships with one another, have the same mindset as Christ Jesus: Who, being in very nature God, did not consider equality with God something to be used to his advantage; rather, he made himself nothing by taking the very nature of a servant, being made in human likeness."

Grandma Lily continues, "Jesus thought it not robbery to be equal to a servant to die for us. That opened the door to a relationship with God and us. After Jesus ascended back into Heaven, The Holy Spirit was sent to comfort and guild us through life. God wants to see us win. He sacrificed His only son just to save us. God gave it all for us, so trust Him with your all, including your problems. The Holy Spirit will then begin to move in your life."

Lily looked at her grandma with unsureness. Lily was the type that had to see it to believe. She wanted to trust her grandma, but the story sounded too good to be true. Grandma Lily noticed that she lost Lily mentally, so she did not want to stress being saved any longer. Grandma Lily left Lily's room and went downstairs to make them a coffee and breakfast. Lily decided to just hang out in her room. She began to read the scriptures her grandma shared with her. She started to read out loud and then paused for a moment. Lily prayed, "Lord, I need you to show me a sign soon because I don't know which way to go at this point in my life. I understand what grandma said, Lord. Could you please give me a little time to figure out what it is I really want, please?" Lily sat down, holding the bible in her hands, hoping to get a revelation. She thought about life long and hard. Lily took out a notebook and began to write. She found herself writing down relationship goals. After Lily filled up a few pages, she thought maybe she had too many standards.

As she erased some of them, she began to cry out to God. "Lord, help me, please. I need you. What do I do, God? I thought I had love all figured out, but apparently not after three heartbreaks in a row," Lily cried with tears rolling down her face. Then a small voice whispered to Lily, "you have searched for many things from men but have not searched for me. You want a man to understand you, shower you with love, and accept you, but they can not give what they do not have. Your quest will end in tears each time until your perspective changes. I am the only one who can give you everything you need and more."

Lily thought she had completely lost her mind since she could hear a voice while unable to see anyone else in the room. It sounded like a man, but she was not afraid. Lily knew there was definitely a voice, but who was he? She thought maybe it was someone in her head. Maybe Lily had gone mad as a result of the heartbreaks? She needed to lay down to gather her thoughts. Lily then thought to herself if she answered the voice back, she could make sense of it all. Lily replied to the small voice, "What do you mean? I have never asked to be hurt. My parents were the first to abandon me, which broke my heart. I did not search or ask for that. How do you explain them leaving me? I know my grandma loves me, but I need more. After trying to make sense of the abandonment of my parents, the men that did me wrong seemed me out. I did not search for them either. Yes, I agreed to date them, but I had no idea they would mishandle me. I did not expect them to treat me like I was nothing. I do not understand how I am the one to blame for my pain. Please help me to understand."

"Lily, you want everyone's approval but mine. I see you are hurt. I know your pain. I bottled up every tear, which turns into liquid gold when I close the lid. Even your tears are special to me. Therefore, I protect them, too, even though you have no clue. I also keep you from harm beyond your sight and understanding because you are special to me," said the small voice. Lily then knew the small voice was God because He is the only one with the power to do such a thing. She was overwhelmed by the experience of God speaking directly to her. "God, you speak as if you know every detail of me," responded Lily in shock.

"My beloved child, I knew you before I formed you in your mother's womb. I planned your life before I breathed life into you. I'm the God that created all things. Nothing is impossible for me to do. Come and walk with me. I'll show you things through the Holy Spirit that man cannot show you. I will take care of you in ways that no man ever could," said The Lord. Lily replied, "God, how do I search for you to get the answers to my prayers? How do I know I am on the right path? The Lord said to Lily, "accept my Son, Jesus Christ, as your Lord and Savior. Repent of your sins, confess that Jesus Christ is Lord, and believe in your heart that I raised Him from the dead. Then by faith, you are saved, and I will work wonders on your behalf." At that moment, Lily remembered the scripture her grandma would read to her from time to time. "For God so loved the world that he gave his one and only Son, that whoever believes in him shall not perish but have eternal life." John 3:16 NIV.

Lily added, "I guess that explains why grandma was so adamant about me learning of you. How do I know you will always love me?" The Lord whispered, "I will never leave you. "Keep your lives free from the love of money and be content with what you have because God has said, "Never will I leave you; never will I forsake you." Hebrews13:5 NIV. Many have left you, but I, the Father, will always be with you."

Lily knew she had been through a lot in a short time and did not want to endure any more brokenness. Therefore, she decided to give God a chance. She realized she needed to put her trust in someone, so why not give Jesus a try. Lily trusted in so many others, and it failed. Therefore, she could not afford to fall again but move forward. Lily submitted her life over to Jesus that day, then her journey began. God gave Lily revelation of who He is in her life every day. They grew in their relationship, and Lily fell in love with The Lord. Lily began telling everyone about Jesus Christ and how He saved her from rejection, abandonment, and heartbreaks that caused her to think about suicide.

She developed an unbreakable trust for God because she surrendered her heart, mind, and soul to Him. Lily realized the love she searched for was lust disguised as love, and they were completely different from one another. God revealed to Lily what love is according to 1 Corinthians13:4-8, 13 NIV, "Love is patient, love is kind. It does not envy, it does not boast, it is not proud. It does not dishonor others, it is not self-seeking, it is not easily angered, it keeps no record of wrongs. Love does not delight in evil but rejoices with the truth. It always protects, always trusts, always hopes, always perseveres. Love never fails. But where there are prophecies, they will cease; where there are tongues, they will be stilled; where there is knowledge, it will pass away. And now these three remain: faith, hope and love. But the greatest of these is love."

We as people don't look for God's love, but God loves us enough that He searches for us instead. Until God grabs hold of us, we believe everyone else and everything else is the answer to our problems. God allows us to go through hurt and pain to draw to Him for help. He gave us free will to choose our direction, and it's up to us to pick wisely. When we do not select the correct option, there are consequences.

"My child, don't reject the Lord's discipline, and don't be upset when he corrects you. For the Lord corrects those he loves, just as a father corrects a child in whom he delights." Proverbs3:11-12 NLT.

God takes care of everything we need because He cares for us. We always complain about His timing and never give God any credit or the credit He deserves for His provision. Did you know God is time! Therefore, He knows when the need has to be supplied. Therefore, appreciate the blessings whenever they happen. Once we get to the place in our lives where we realize God is all we will ever need, our lives will be so much easier. We can no longer only chase God when we need Him or when it's convenient for us. We must search for Him continually. Stop putting God in a box on a shelf for Him to await our arrival as if we are The Master.

The moral of the story is that no matter how much we search for love, we will never find it until we encounter Jesus. God is the only one who will love us unconditionally because He is love! So, if you are looking for love, change the direction of your perspective and search for Jesus because He is the way and truth.

MACK
MOVES HOUSE
Written by
Rachel Newhouse
Illustrated by
Patrick Smith

To "my boys" Zeke and Gabe. I'm so proud of you. —RN